fatty legs

A True Story

fatty legs

Christy JORDAN-FENTON *&*
Margaret POKIAK-FENTON

Artwork by Liz Amini-Holmes

annick press
toronto + new york + vancouver

Annick Press Ltd.

Edited by Maggie DeVries
Copyedited by Pam Robertson
Proofread by Laura Edlund
Cover and interior design by Lisa Hemingway
Cover and interior illustrations by Liz Amini-Holmes

Cataloging in Publication
Jordan, Christy
    Fatty legs / Christy Jordan-Fenton and Margaret Pokiak-Fenton ;
    artwork by Liz Amini-Holmes.

ISBN 978-1-55451-247-8 (bound).—ISBN 978-1-55451-246-1 (pbk.)

1. Fenton, Margaret Lucy—Childhood and youth—Juvenile literature. 2. Inuit—
Canada—Residential schools—Juvenile literature. 3. Inuit women—Biography—
Juvenile literature. I. Fenton, Margaret Lucy II. Amini-Holmes, Liz III. Title.

E96.5.J65 2010   J371.829'9712071   C2010-901180-5

We acknowledge the support of the Canada Council for the Arts, the Ontario Arts
Council, and the Government of Canada through the Book Publishing Industry
Development Program (BPIDP) for our publishing activities.

ONTARIO ARTS COUNCIL
CONSEIL DES ARTS DE L'ONTARIO

Printed and bound in China.

Published in the U.S.A. by
Annick Press (U.S.) Ltd.

Distributed in Canada by
Firefly Books Ltd.
66 Leek Crescent
Richmond Hill, ON
L4B 1H1

Distributed in the U.S.A. by
Firefly Books (U.S.) Inc.
P.O. Box 1338
Ellicott Station
Buffalo, NY 14205

VISIT OUR WEBSITE AT WWW.ANNICKPRESS.COM

FOR MY THREE LITTLE INSPIRATIONS—Qugyuk, Aklak, and Paniktuaq—and their loving father, my husband, Garth. None of this would have been possible without your patience. For Penny Howe, my grade 7/8 teacher: thank you for sharing with a young girl that people as fantastic as you came from the same place as people like me. For Brad Hawranik, my first section commander: I still think of you as one of the finest role models I have ever known. And, for Margaret: you have given us a powerful gift. Thank you for being brave enough to share your story.

—*Christy*

FOR MY LATE HUSBAND, LYLE, who helped me to work through the many fears I carried with me from residential school. Your love gave me courage. And, for our children, their husbands and wives, and our many grandchildren.

—*Margaret*

Olemaun, who was later called Margaret, at home on
Banks Island. Here she stands (on the right) with two of
her younger sisters, Elizabeth and Mabel.

Introduction

MY NAME IS OLEMAUN POKIAK—that's
OO-*lee-mawn*—but some of my classmates
used to call me "Fatty Legs." They called me that
because a wicked nun forced me to wear a pair of red
stockings that made my legs look enormous. But I put
an end to it. How? Well, I am going to let you in on
a secret that I have kept for more than 60 years: the
secret of how I made those stockings disappear.

Beaufort Sea

ALASKA

Sachs Harbour

BANKS ISLAND

Tuktoyaktuk

Baillie Islands

Aklavik

Reindeer Station

RICHARDSON MOUNTAINS

Peel River

Mackenzie River

NORTHWEST
TERRITORIES

VICTORIA
ISLAND

YUKON
TERRITORY

Great
Bear
Lake

NUNAVUT

Margaret's route to school ••••

Chapter ONE

WHEN I WAS A YOUNG GIRL, outsiders came flitting about the North. They plucked us from our homes on the scattered islands of the Arctic Ocean and carried us back to the nests they called schools, in Aklavik.

Three times I had made the five-day journey to Aklavik with my father, across the open ocean, past Tuktoyaktuk, and through the tangled Mackenzie River delta, to buy supplies. I was mesmerized on each trip by the spectacle of the strange dark-cloaked

See photo on page 88.

nuns, whose tongues flickered with French-Canadian accents, and the pale-skinned priests who had traveled across a different ocean from a far-off land called Belgium. They held the key to the greatest of the outsiders' mysteries—reading.

See photo on page 88.

My older half-sister, Ayouniq, had been plucked before I was born, but we called her "Rosie" after her return. She would tell me nothing about the school tucked away in the maze of the delta, where she had gone for four years, but when I was seven she did read to me from a collection of beautifully colored books my father had given her for Christmas. The stories were precious treasures to be enjoyed in the well-lit, toasty warmth of our smoke-scented tent, as the darkness of winter was constant, and the temperatures outside were cold enough to freeze bare skin in seconds. The books were written in English, so I understood very little of them. I was always left with many unanswered questions.

"What's a rabbit?" I asked Rosie in our language, Inuvialuktun.

"It's like a hare," she told me, lifting her eyes from

Alice's Adventures in Wonderland.

"Oh. Well, why did Alice follow it down the hole? To hunt it?"

Rosie gave me a funny look. "No, Olemaun. She followed it because she was curious."

I tried to imagine being Alice, as the large cook-stove crackled behind me. She was brave to go into that long, dark tunnel, all for curiosity.

"What was it like?"

Rosie looked up from the book again. "What was what like?"

"The outsiders' school."

"I don't know. You ask too many questions," she

said. Her face grew dark in the light of the coal oil lamp. She closed the book and looked away.

"It must have been exciting to live with the outsiders."

She shrugged her shoulders and dropped the book on the table.

"But they taught you how to read…"

Rosie was silent.

"Please," I begged, tugging at her leg as she got up from the table and slipped on her Mother Hubbard parka.

"They cut our hair because our mothers weren't there to braid it for us."

"I don't need my mother to braid my hair. I can do it myself."

"They'd cut it anyway. They always cut the little ones' hair."

"I'm not that little."

"They don't care. They don't have the patience to wait for you to braid your hair. They want all of your time for chores and for kneeling on your knees to ask forgiveness."

"Oh, well. It's only hair."

"It isn't just your hair, Olemaun. They take everything,"

Mother Hubbard parka: the traditional parka worn by Inuvialuit women of the western Arctic.

she said, slipping her feet inside her kamik.

"Well, can you at least finish reading me the story?"

Rosie gave me an icy look. "You want to know about the school so much, you can go there and learn to read for yourself." She turned, pulled apart the flaps of the tent door, and disappeared through the tunnel in the snow that formed the entrance to our home. I ran after her down the dark corridor, but she was already gone into the pitch-black afternoon of the Arctic winter. She knew that our father would not let me go to school. He had told the outsiders "No" the past four summers they had come for me. Rosie was lucky that her aunt had allowed her to go.

See photo on page 89.

ONE DAY AT THE end of February 1944, when the sun had just begun to return to the sky, my father took me hunting with him. We traveled by dogsled for several hours, until we came to a place where game was plentiful.

"Father," I said when we finally stopped, "can I go to the school this year?"

kamik/kamak: a type of boot worn by the Inuit. Also called mukluks.

"No," he said.

"But you and Rosie both went, and I will be eight in June when the ice melts."

He raised his hand, silencing me, and motioned for me to return to the dogsled. Atop a distant hill stood a wolf, its silhouette stark in the afternoon twilight. My father had it in the sights of his rifle. A shot cracked through the air, killing my chance to convince him.

When he returned to the dogsled with the wolf carcass, his knit brow and hard eyes told me that he was finished discussing the matter. I cringed under the cold flash of defeat, but I was careful not to talk any further about my desire to go to school. Instead, I held it inside all through the long months that followed.

See photo on page 89.

My father rarely spoke of the school and would never tell me of the wonderful things I could learn there. He was a smart man who loved to read, but he put little value in the outsiders' learning compared to the things that our people knew.

But my heart would not give up hope. I climbed the cemetery hill and stared out over the sleeping, stone-still water each day, waiting for the sea to come

alive with waves. Sometimes, I brought the book with me, the one about the girl named Alice who followed the hare-like creature down the burrow. I looked at the pictures and remembered the tea party she had, and how her body had become small and large again. But I still did not know what happened to her at the end of that burrow. Did she catch the hare?

IN LATE MAY, WHEN the sun stood constant watch in the sky and night traversed it only briefly like the shadow of a passing bird's wing, I found my father preparing the hides of animals he had collected from his trapline. I knew the topic was forbidden, but I could not silence my heart another day. I asked him once again to allow me to go to school.

"The outsiders do not teach you how to hunt," he said, pointing his knife at the fox he was about to skin. "They only use your knowledge of making snares for their own profit and send you to gather the animals from *their* traplines. They do not teach you how to cure meat and clean fish so that you can live off of the

See photo on page 90.

land. They feed you cabbage soup and porridge. They do not teach you how to make parkas and kamik," he said, eyeing the beautifully crafted Delta braid on my parka and the embroidered, fur-lined boots on my feet. "They make you wear their scratchy outsiders' clothes, which keep out neither the mosquitoes nor the cold. They teach you their songs and dances instead of your own. And they tell you that the spirit inside of you is bad and needs their forgiveness."

I had already learned a lot about hunting, trapping, and curing foods. My friend Agnes, who was 10, had already gone to the school. She told me that the nuns made you sew all of the time. It would not be difficult to learn to sew parkas and kamik if I was used to sewing all of the time. And how could I ever forget our songs and our dances? They were a part of me. But I had once heard the outsiders' beautiful chants resonating from the church in Tuktoyaktuk, and I dreamed of learning to make such music. I would be careful to stay out of trouble, and no one would say I had to kneel and ask forgiveness. They would see that my spirit was good.

Delta braid: a decoration made by cutting patterns from long strips of fabric and layering them on each other; used to decorate Mother Hubbard parkas.

I would be patient, but I would not give up. I would wait and ask my father again.

Time melted away. My eighth birthday came and went. The sea began to wake from its slumber, and I knew it would not be long before the ice broke from the shore and was carried out to be swallowed by the ocean. Soon all of us—my father and the other hunters and trappers, along with their families—would leave our winter home on Banks Island to carry boatloads of pelts to Aklavik. The outsiders had many islands to scour for children during the short summer season, and ours was a long distance from Aklavik. As it was so far for them to travel, it was unlikely that we would be there when they came. My father was my only hope.

One day in late June, I looked up from staring at the book I was so desperate to read and saw that the enormous splintering chunks of ice had left enough of a gap to allow us passage. I slammed the book shut, sped down the hill, and ran along the rocky shore as fast as I could—which was fast, because my legs were muscular and strong. I was determined and ready to ask again. "Father, Father, please, Father… *Pleeease,* can I go to school this year?" I huffed in heavy breaths, darting through the small groups of men who were loading the schooners for the journey.

My father heaved a bale of white fox pelts over the edge of the *North Star.* His answer had not changed: "No."

"Please, please, *pleeease,*" I begged. "You can drop me at Aklavik when you go for supplies."

My father paused to swat a mosquito. He looked into my eyes. "You are a stubborn girl," he told me, "and the outsiders do not like stubborn children."

"Please," I said again. "Please."

He crouched to my height. He picked up a rock with one of his hands and held it out to me. "Do you see this rock? It was once jagged and full of sharp, jutting points, but the water of the ocean slapped and slapped at it, carrying away its angles and edges. Now it is nothing but a small pebble. That is what the outsiders will do to you at the school."

"But Father, the water did not change the stone inside the rock. Besides, I am not a rock. I am a girl,

schooner: a type of sailing vessel with masts.   13

I can move. I am not stuck upon the shore for eternity."

"You are a clever one," he said, touching my cheek and then looking down at the book in my hand.

"Does that mean I can go?" My hope blossomed, billowing beneath my parka.

He looked deep into my eyes, the rock held tightly in his fist. "I suppose it is the only way I will hear the end of it."

I turned to run and tell my mother the news, but my father reached for me and pulled me in. He held me in his arms for a long time, the fur of his parka pressed against my face, so that I could hardly breathe. When he finally let go, I did not give him a single moment to change his mind. Even faster than I had run to the shore, I ran back up to my mother, who was in our tent packing up the belongings we would need for the journey.

"Mother, Mother!" I shouted as I rushed through the entrance. "Father says I can go to school this year!"

She did not say a word. Instead, she set my little sister down on a caribou hide, pushed past me out of the tent, and headed straight for him.

I could tell she did not think it was such terrific news.

See photo on page 90.

Chapter TWO

THE SCHOONERS WERE FULL to the gunwales with a winter's worth of pelts for trading. Everything we needed for the trip had been packed from our tents. The men used long poles to pry the boats free of the shore, where they were stored for the winter, and a system of pulleys to pull them back into the water. Planks were laid down to bridge the gap between the shore and the schooners, and we all climbed aboard and prepared for our spring migration.

Stefansson expedition: the Arctic expedition of 1913 to 1916, organized by Vilhjalmur Stefansson, a Canadian explorer of Icelandic descent.

We traveled with six other schooners, each carrying as many as six or seven families. Our schooner was the *North Star.* It was owned by Mr. Carpenter and Mr. Wolki, but had once been part of the famous Stefansson expedition's fleet. We stayed aboard the ships for the entire five-day journey.

See photo on page 91.

Five days may not seem like much, but to me it might as well have been a year. From the first day, I searched for signs that we were nearing the mainland. The voyage across the ocean was fraught with anticipation, and when we finally reached Tuktoyaktuk, I felt both happiness that we had made it that far and sadness that we still had a long way to go. Beyond Tuktoyaktuk, the pingos rose out of the ocean like goose eggs with smashed-in tops. We passed them and entered the mouth of the Mackenzie River. The Richardson Mountains cut into the horizon far off to the southwest, and small, sparse trees lined the shores. We came to Reindeer Station, a settlement of herders, and excitement consumed me. We would soon be heading up the Peel River, the last leg of our journey.

See photo on page 91.

See photo on page 92.

Sometime after lunch, on the final day, the noise

pingos: when ice forms in the ground during winter months, it pushes the surface earth up into small hills, or pingos, which grow bigger year after year. The name pingo comes from the Inuvialuktun word for small hill.

of children playing reached our ears, and we could see spiraling towers of smoke rising high into the sky from many campfires. A dozen boats as large as whales were tethered to the bank. We had made it! We had reached Aklavik!

After our schooner was secured and a large board was laid over the side of the *North Star,* we children were given permission to go and seek out our friends and cousins, who had also arrived to sell their pelts and stock up on supplies for the year. We made our way down the plank and scrambled up the steep muddy slope to the settlement our own great-grandfather, Old Man Pokiak, had founded as a trading post.

See photo on page 92.

LATER THAT DAY, AFTER my father had sold his winter's catch of furs, my mother came to find me. I was giddy with excitement, knowing what was to come. I tossed the caribou-hide ball I was playing with high into the air, leaving a cluster of children scrambling for it, as I followed my mother to the Hudson's Bay Company. The Hudson's Bay Company

Hudson's Bay Company: the oldest surviving company in North America, incorporated by a royal charter in 1670. Hunters and trappers traded their pelts there for goods and supplies.

was a magical place. They sold everything a person could ever need, from furniture to ladies' dresses, from rifles to candy.

See photo on page 93.

My mother stopped me on the stairs before I could race into the small treasure-packed timber building. She took one of my long braids in her hand. "You know, the nuns will cut your hair. Are you sure you still want to attend the school?"

"Yes," I told her and tried to make my face very serious.

"They will make you work hard. Harder than you do when you help your father."

"I am strong," I said, pushing my shoulders back.

"They will not be kind to you. They are not your family, and they are not like us."

"I will have Agnes. I will be fine. You will see."

My mother sure seemed to know a lot about a place she had never been. I figured she was trying to scare me. Life would be more difficult without me there to help her with the smaller children, and she was likely jealous of my opportunity to learn to read.

"Well then, we had better go in and find you some

new stockings to keep your legs warm underneath your uniform."

My mother bought me some strange-smelling soap, a comb to keep my hair neat, a brush for my teeth, and something in a white tube. She also bought me a thick, heavy pair of gray stockings. They were like the kind I had seen the outsiders wear, the kind that pull up above your knees. I wanted to put them on right away, but my mother told me I had to wait. I would not want to soil them before school, because the outsiders loved cleanliness.

As we left the store, I noticed a member of the RCMP relaxing on a chair near the entrance. The Mountie was reading from one of the many richly colored books that crammed a tall column of shelves beside him. How distinguished he looked as he pulled at a pipe, a book in his hand. Soon, I, too, would be able to read.

MY PARENTS DID NOT let me go to school right away. They wanted to keep me until after the athletic

RCMP or Mounties: Royal Canadian Mounted Police. Canada's national police force.

games, which were held on Dominion Day, the first
of July—three whole days after our arrival. July was a
festive time of year for the Inuit, including us Inuvialuit,
and for the Dene Nation, made up of native peoples
such as the Gwich'in. Freed at last from the ice, the
men would bring their families to Aklavik not only
for supplies, but to also compete against each other in

Dominion Day: Canada's national holiday, now
known as Canada Day, which is celebrated on July 1.

21

tests of strength. I was disappointed that I could not go to school immediately, but I did not often get to see my cousins and enjoyed visiting with them.

On the first day of the games, my father made a balloon for us by blowing up the sac from the throat of a ptarmigan. We chased each other down a long, seemingly endless street, the sound of our feet clomping and thudding against the wooden boardwalk, batting the balloon into the air and stealing it from one another. I caught it and ran. Soon I could no longer hear my sisters and cousins behind me. I had lost them.

I looked up and stopped, forgetting the balloon.

In front of me, at least a dozen children dressed in uniforms crouched in a silty garden, breaking the earth and pulling at roots with small tools. These had to be the naughty children who were made to kneel for forgiveness. Behind them stood two immense wooden buildings, so much larger than our schooner, with rows and rows of windows. I had forgotten how big these buildings were.

This was where I would go to school, but I would not be like these children. I would be good and spend

ptarmigan: white game birds of the grouse family and the official bird of Nunavut, a territory in Canada. Also known as snow chickens.

all of my time inside, learning to read. I batted the balloon from one hand to the other, and turned and ran back to find my cousins and my sisters.

The day after the athletic games began, a boat docked. We watched its passengers file up the beach. They were children with solemn faces, some of them crying. I searched the faces for Agnes, but she was not among them.

See photo on page 93.

"See those children," my mother said to me. "They will be your classmates."

"Why are they crying?" I asked.

"Because they do not want to go to the outsiders' school."

"Don't they know they are going to learn to read?"

"They would rather be with their families than read," my mother said, tightening her lips. Her words stung.

"Now that the other new children are here, it is time for us to take you to the school," my father said, coming up behind us. "Go and gather your things."

MY PARENTS LED ME along the same street I had run down to lose my sisters and cousins, the day before. The buildings came into view. The garden was deserted now.

"Are they both schools?" I asked my father.

"No. Only that one." He pointed at the building on the right. "The other is the hospital where you will be trained when you are old enough. You may be asked to help out there at times."

"Like a nurse? That sounds fun."

My father gave me a look that said he did not think so. "The top floor is where the students sleep. The building is divided into a boys' side and a girls' side, and you will not be allowed to talk with the boys, even if they are your cousins."

The school was beginning to look less inviting. I wondered how I would ever feel safe enough to sleep in such a large place. I was used to staring at the glowing coals of my father's pipe, from where I slept under his bed, until I drifted off. It suddenly sank in. My family would not be staying with me. How would I fall asleep without that smoky red glow?

"The church is in the middle of the dorm rooms, and the classrooms and refectory are below them," he explained.

"What is a refectory?"

"A place where many people eat together."

My mother was silent. She did not say a word until my father had his hand on the big double doors of the school. "It is not too late to change your mind, Olemaun."

Change my mind? I could manage. I would read myself to sleep like Rosie did. I wasn't going to let anything stop me. I couldn't wait to go inside.

My father placed a hand on my shoulder. "You will not be able to return home for a very long time."

"I know," I said, but I didn't.

My eighth birthday had only just passed. I did not yet understand how long a year was. It had not crossed my mind that the same ice that allowed my people to travel only in the brief weeks of summer would keep me from going home. I did not know that an unusually short summer in 1945 would hold me prisoner for a second year with the Sisters, the Fathers, and the Brothers. They were not family; they were like owls and ravens raising wrens.

See photo on page 94.

My father pulled open the door, and I stepped past him. I was inside a school for the first time in my life. All around me was glass and wood. An enormous photograph hung on one of the clean, painted walls. In it, an outsider wore a fancy sash. Medallions like large coins hung from his chest—I would learn later that he was the king of all of the outsiders. They told

me he was also my king, but I knew that my family listened to no one but Mr. Carpenter and Mr. Wolki, who owned the *North Star*. The school's smells were unfriendly and harsh against the tender skin of my inner nostrils. I craned my head in every possible direction I could, without moving my feet. It was like someone had enlarged the Hudson's Bay Company by many times and stripped it clean. My eyes darted from wall to wall, trying to take it all in.

An outsider with a hooked nose like a beak came for me, her scraping footsteps echoing through the long, otherwise silent halls. "I am glad you have come to your senses," she told my father in Inuvialuktun. "*You* certainly can't teach her the things she needs to know." She wrapped a dark-cloaked arm around my shoulder and ushered me away, without giving me a chance to say goodbye. I looked back and saw my father wiping tears from my mother's face. I wanted to run to her and tell her that it would be all right, but a priest approached them right then and they walked away with him.

Chapter THREE

I FOLLOWED THE BEAKED NUN up stairs that creaked under my feet to a large room filled with beds. Across the room were seven girls, who had been among the sullen children I had seen earlier. They were standing in a somber line in front of four foul-smelling, wooden stalls along one wall. The outsider pushed me into place at the end of the row, and I nearly gagged from the odor that wafted from the stalls behind us.

Another dark-cloaked nun passed by the girls,
eyeing them up and down, one by one. She clutched
a large pair of shears. She stopped in front of a small
sickly looking Inuit girl. I knew the girl must be of the
Copper Inuit from Victoria Island, because her parka
cover was drawn high at the sides, the front and back
hanging low like a beaver's tail, unlike the Mother
Hubbard parkas we wore in the west. The girl shrank
under the nun's glare. Catching a firm hold on one
of the girl's long braids, the nun snipped it off with a

Inuit: a general term for the Aboriginal peoples—including the Inuvialiut and
Copper Inuit—who inhabit the Arctic regions of Canada, Greenland, Russia, and
the United States. The term "Inuit" has largely replaced "Eskimo."

clean slice and let it fall to the floor. The girl hid her face in her hands as the second braid was cut.

The nun did the same to four other girls, sparing only one older girl and one of the outsiders' children, who was likely a trapper's daughter. The sound of the shears severing thick black hair drowned out the howls of the disgraced girls.

At last, only I remained. I held my breath. I was large for my age. Surely she would pass over me.

She did not. She stopped directly in front of me. I stepped back from her heavy cross, which nearly struck me in the face, but she reached out and yanked me back by one braid.

"I can fix my own hair," I protested in Inuvialuktun, but she held tight and, with the same motion a bird makes to pull a piece of flesh from a fish, clamped the jaws of the shears down on my braid and severed it. I was horrified. I wasn't a baby. My other braid fell to the floor to meet the first, and I joined the others in their weeping.

There we stood, sobbing in the humiliation of our discarded hair.

A tall Gwich'in girl in a
uniform came into the room.
She gave a comforting look to
one of the weeping girls, who I
knew to also be Gwich'in by the
wraparound moccasins she wore.
My mother had warned me about the Gwich'in. They
were not like us Inuvialuit and did not get along with
our people. The uniformed girl looked at me. A thin,
malicious smile crinkled her lips.

I wished they would cut her hair, too.

She was joined by three other braided girls in uniforms. One of the nuns said something to them that I
did not understand. They marched out the door and
returned, moments later, with their arms full. I looked
for Agnes among them, as they scurried between us
passing out the impractical clothes that we were to
wear. They had us exchange our warm, comfortable
kamik and moccasins for outsider-shoes, and issued
each of us a short-sleeved blouse and two pinafores,
one navy blue and one khaki. But the worst were the
scratchy canvas bloomers. They expected us to wear

underwear made out of the same stuff that tents were made with. They knew nothing of living in the North, nor how to dress for it.

The hook-nosed nun shrieked something. I had no idea what she was saying. She held her bony finger out, pointing it directly at me. The floorboards of the dormitory groaned, and I held my breath, scared of what might come next. From a distance, a familiar voice whispered, "Change into the new clothes."

I turned, and there was Agnes. She had come in and joined the other uniformed girls. One of the nuns hurried over to her, a harsh rasp flying from her mouth. I felt bad that Agnes had gotten into trouble for speaking to me, but I was glad she was there. I gave her a hint of a smile and began to dress.

I hated my new clothes. I was much larger than the other girls my age, and the clothes did not fit well. The shoes pinched my feet. The bottoms were hard and stiff. They did not form to the shape of my foot like I was used to, and there was no padding inside of them. The faded, black secondhand stockings were as transparent as walrus intestines and much too small. They

Yup'ik: the Inuit who live in western and central Alaska and at the easternmost point of Russia.

did not reach to the elastic bottoms of my bloomers, so I had no way of holding them up. It was a good thing my mother had bought me my own stockings. I reached into my bag and pulled them out, but the nun snatched them from me with a scaly claw. I stood up straight, hands on my hips, and let out a huff.

"And who do you think you are?" she asked me in my own language.

"I am Olemaun Pokiak," I told her, puffing my chest.

"We use our Christian names here. And we speak English." She narrowed her eyes. "You are Margaret," she said, switching languages.

She could say what she wanted—I knew what my grandfather had named me. It was Olemaun, the same as his Alaskan-Yup'ik mother, and it meant the hard stone that is used to sharpen an ulu. But I could not tell her, because I did not speak nearly enough English. Nor could I do anything about my clothing, though I knew my knees would play peek-a-boo with the cold when I walked, and my toes would freeze as they poked holes through the ends of my onionskin tights. Why would she not just let me wear my own stockings?

ulu: a knife with a rocker-like blade, traditionally used by Inuit women for tasks such as scraping hides, cutting hair, and preparing food.

35

The nun scuttled to the wall facing the stalls. With one long bony hand, she picked up a cloth from a shelf that was lined with washbasins and made a circular motion with it in front of her face. She pretended to scrub behind her ears and under her armpits. I didn't need a lesson on how to wash my face. I already knew how to do that. What I needed was to learn how to read.

After she finished her class on washing, she opened her mouth and let out a squawk. First, the outsider's daughter took out a tube and a toothbrush from among her belongings. The rest of us did as she did. I placed some paste from the tube on the end of my toothbrush, and stuck it in my mouth. It was worse than a fly's breakfast. I couldn't help but gag and spit it out. The raven-like nun called out "Katherine," and the Gwich'in girl who had smiled when my hair was cut tore the tube from my hand and took it to her. The nun cackled and held the tube up for the other girls to see. The older ones laughed loudly, especially the Gwich'in girl called Katherine. The Gwich'in always thought they were better than us.

A tall slender nun appeared in the doorway. She was pale and seemed to float across the bathroom floor. She turned to the Raven, seeking an explanation for the commotion.

I could hardly take my eyes off her.

The Raven made a gesture from her cheekbone to her jaw, like a man shaving his whiskers. The new girls now laughed, too.

My mother had bought that tube for me. They were not just laughing at me. They were laughing at her. I wanted to tell the nun that it was not funny. My mother could not read. How was she to know that she was buying shaving cream and not toothpaste?

I saw the muscles of the tall nun's beautiful, long neck tense, but she did not laugh. She glided toward me and pulled a small tube from her pocket.

I am not trying that, I thought. *I have had enough of the outsiders' pastes.*

She took a drop from the tube, placed it on her own tongue, and smiled. After rinsing my brush, she put a strip of the paste on it. "Mmm," she said.

I trusted her smile, so I put it in my mouth. It was cool and refreshing like the mints my father had once bought us at the Hudson's Bay Company. As I ran the brush across my teeth, I could see the tall nun in the mirror. She looked like a pale swan, long and elegant. Later, Agnes told me that her name was Sister MacQuillan, and that she was in charge of all of the other nuns. She would be the perfect woman to teach me how to read, but reading, as I discovered, would have to wait.

Once we had finished cleaning ourselves, it was time to clean the school. We were separated into groups. I was lucky: I was put into Agnes's group. We were assigned to clean one of the classrooms. We wiped down the desks, the walls, and the floor with a harsh-smelling liquid that made our eyes water and ate at the skin on our fingers.

After we had dusted, swept, and washed everything, we rubbed wax into the wood floor until it was as smooth and as slick as ice. Agnes and the other girls had fun slipping and sliding around on it, but my stockings were too worn on the bottoms for sliding. I perched myself in one of the small wooden desks to see how it would feel. Letters, like those from Rosie's books, decorated the walls of the classroom. I stared at them, trying to decipher what they might mean.

See photo on page 94.

Suddenly, the girls fell silent. I turned to see why. *WHAP!* A stick came down on the desk I was sitting in. I jumped in my skin. The Raven stood over me, with a look that made it clear she did not approve of me sitting down. I scrambled to my feet. She shoved a dusting cloth in my hand and pointed to the rows and rows of books at the back of the class. The other girls were dismissed to get ready for dinner, but I had to stay.

By the end of my first day, the only books I had touched were the ones I dusted.

I HARDLY SLEPT THAT night. The bed had a rickety frame that creaked every time I took a breath. Each girl's bed was as loud as mine, and the noise filled the vast space of the large room with a disjointed foreign sound, unlike the sleepy rhythmic breathing of my mother, father, and siblings, with whom I had shared a tent since birth. Sobs also carried through the room. My eiderdown blanket was soft, but I missed the musky smell of furry hides, the comforting aroma of smoke drifting through the air, and the darkness of the tent, even in summer. The thin serge curtain above my bed did little to keep the midnight sun from penetrating the huge room. Gathering the blanket off my assigned bed, I crawled underneath it, squinted my eyes, and imagined that my father's pipe was glowing in the distance.

They woke us very early the next morning, but my sleep had been almost as brief as the short-lived darkness. By the time the nuns entered the room, clapping their hands fiercely, I was dressed and seated on the edge of my bed. I was not about to let another minute stand between me and my chance to learn.

However, all I was about to learn was what was to be
done with the smelly buckets I had discovered in the
stalls, the night before. We called them honey buckets,
but there was nothing sweet about a bucket that was
used as a toilet. With extreme care, we hauled them
down the stairs and across the school yard, where we
dumped them in the river. When we returned, we
were set to work cleaning the chicken coop. A long
time passed before we were herded back upstairs
and given a few minutes to attend to our hygiene.
My stomach ached with hunger and my mind ached
for knowledge. I could not wait to go to Sister
MacQuillan's class and begin reading.

See photo on page 95.

After we were inspected for cleanliness, we were led in single file into a strange room that separated the boys' and girls' dormitories. It was filled with long benches, instead of desks, but there were books placed along them. At last, I would learn to read. Standing at the head of the room was the priest who had taken my parents away the day before. I spotted Sister MacQuillan in the front row, but she did not get up to teach us. Instead, the nuns came around and made us get down on our knees and hang our heads. It seemed like an odd way to learn anything. Agnes saw my confusion and whispered to me in Inuvialuktun, "We are supposed to pray for our souls."

I nodded my head and prayed to start class soon.

My prayers were not answered.

After kneeling, we were taken to eat a breakfast of soggy, bland, mushy oatmeal. Each bowl was sprinkled with a scant teaspoon of brown sugar, which hardly disguised the revolting, tasteless stuff.

I wondered how Agnes, who was sitting next to me, could eat it with such enthusiasm.

"You get used to it," she said, shrugging her shoulders.

"Really? So, do we learn to read after breakfast?"

Agnes put down her spoon and turned to face me. Her face was sad and sympathetic. "Oh, no, we will not begin classes until the ice freezes again in the fall."

I stared at her, horror replacing hunger in my belly. My spirit sank like the stockings that slouched around my ankles.

Why had I been so eager to come here? I thought of my sisters and cousins. They were still in Aklavik, nearly within shouting distance. I wanted to yell to them to wake my father and tell him to come and get me so that I could spend the day dancing and watching the games.

"What do we do, until then?" I asked her, fearing the answer.

"We do chores, and we play."

I had spent so many days anticipating the thaw, and now I would spend my days scrubbing, gathering wood, and mending uniforms, impatiently waiting for the freeze.

Chapter FOUR

THE SUMMER TOOK AN eternity to pass, but
eventually it did. I was working outside one day
when the last of the outsiders' boats returned to
Aklavik carrying both freshly plucked children and
those they had regathered. We saw them make their
way past us, where we knelt in the garden.

"We will start classes tomorrow," Agnes told me. I
felt like dancing around the potatoes, but the Raven
was watching me, and I didn't dare.

Walking into the classroom the next morning, I stood as straight as I could. I was hoping to impress Sister MacQuillan, but I was in for a shock. The kind nun wasn't there. It was the Raven who hovered behind the large wooden desk, where Sister MacQuillan should have been. How could the Raven be my teacher? The smile shrank from my face as I squeezed into the small desk that she pointed me to. Unfortunately, it was right in front of hers. After all of the other children had been seated, she let out a croak. By now, most of us who were new had become very good at following the cues of the older girls. We had even learned a few phrases of English.

Each of us found a reader inside of our desk. We pulled the books out and set them before us. The Raven rose from her seat, closing in on me, and pointed a yard stick in my direction, motioning for me to stand.

"She wants you to read aloud," whispered Agnes from the seat behind me.

I rose to my feet, but how was I to read? I didn't even know which page to turn to.

See photo on page 95.

The Raven cocked her hip and tapped a foot. *"Welllll?"* she said.

My cheeks felt hot. I looked around me, from child to child. The faces stared back, blank, waiting, as my stockings began to slide down my calves.

The Gwich'in girl raised her hand high into the air.

"Katherine," acknowledged the nun.

She rose and started reading aloud from her own schoolbook.

The Raven raised a wing-like arm, silencing Katherine. She turned back to me and pointed her finger to the ground.

The other children giggled.

"You can sit down now," Agnes said in a soft voice.

How did the Raven expect us to learn without speaking to us in our language, so we could understand?

My first reading lesson had not been what I had anticipated. I was grateful when it was over, and I launched myself from my desk, eager to follow the others outside to play. But the Raven stopped me. She put a brush in my hand and pointed to the colossal chalkboards. I gave her a questioning look. I did

46

not know why she was making me stay to clean them. She answered with something in English that I did not comprehend, and my older class-mates cried with laughter as they left the room.

Later, I stopped Agnes in the hall.

"What did the teacher say that made the others laugh at the end of class?" I asked.

"She said that cleaning the boards should be no problem for you, because you are so tall your stock-ings won't even stay up."

"She has it in for me. I know she does."

"Who?" asked a lyrical voice in our own language. It was Sister MacQuillan. We had not noticed that we were standing in front of her office.

"No one, Sister," answered Agnes, in English, before tugging me down the hall.

THE RAVEN THOUGHT SHE knew a lot, but she cared more about making us do chores than about teaching us. She said that chores were part of our education. For some reason, she seemed to think that I needed more of an education than the others, and as the weeks went by, I was forever mopping the floors, tidying the recreation room, and emptying the honey buckets. I wasn't sure what she meant to teach me, but I had something to teach her about the spirit of us Inuvialuit.

See photo on page 96.

ONE EVENING IN OCTOBER, after a hard day of the Raven's education, I sat over my bowl of cabbage soup in the long dining hall, watching the other children eat. It was the same food we had been force-fed when we first arrived, and I remembered how many girls had become ill. Those same girls were now lapping it up, because they were starving. It made me angry. How could they expect us to eat this meatless mush? My father's sled dogs would not have licked the bowl it was put in. My stomach hurt, but that night I refused to touch it to my lips.

"Perhaps you need help with your appetite," suggested the Raven as she dropped a soppy wet rag right in my lap. She didn't have to say another word. By now, I knew that she intended for me to wipe down all of the tables.

I looked to Katherine and the other Gwich'in girls. They were like a flock of open-mouthed hatchlings, giggling at me.

"If I had a pocket of stones, I would shoo you with a storm of pebbles," I said, and pushed the rag to the floor.

That Raven swooped down and clutched my dress in her claw. "This is no place for a willful child," she hissed.

I jerked back, knocking my bowl over.

The mush oozed down the Raven's dark habit. This time the hatchlings were laughing at her. She raised her claw at me and I crouched to avoid the blow. Then

Sister MacQuillan glided between us, the Swan protecting me with her gentle wing.

The Raven fixed her sharp little eyes on me for a long moment before scuttling off to clean herself up.

The refectory had long since been deserted by the time I made it to the last table. A dark shadow grew in the doorway. It was the Raven. "You seem to require a little more education!" she whispered.

I knew I was in for trouble.

Chapter FIVE

I WAS A GOOD STUDENT despite the Raven's cruelty. I looked at it as a game and practiced harder at reading, writing, and arithmetic than any other girl in my class. Not only did I enjoy proving my teacher wrong, but I figured I had to learn as much as I could that year, because I planned to leave on the *North Star* with my parents the next summer and never return. While my schoolmates played cards and made dolls during their recreation time, I chose to read. I started with the simple readers we were given,

See photo on page 96.

tracing my finger over the words again and again, trying to sound them out and decipher what they meant, but by spring I was reading books like the ones that Rosie had. I bided my time and waited to escape the Raven.

When the first boats began to appear, I could hardly believe the time had come. It would not be long before my parents arrived. However, on one of the boats was a letter from my father. The *North Star*, along with the other schooners, had not made it home to Banks Island the summer before. They had been stranded on a smaller island by an early freeze. The hunting and trapping had not been as successful there, and the entire group had decided to do their trading in Tuktoyaktuk instead of coming all the way to Aklavik, for fear of being caught by the ice again.

See photo on page 97.

I was devastated. This could not be happening. By now I could read and knew my times tables as well as Katherine, and I was ready to go home. It was

time—and my parents
were not going to come
for me. Not sure if they
would ever come for me,
I cried until the letter
was so soaked with tears,
it tore in my hands. That
night I had a nightmare.
I dreamed I was locked
beneath the Raven's habit
with many other children.
She cackled and laughed as we tried to break free,
straining against its weight, knowing that we would
never see our parents again.

Outside, men competed in athletics and women
gossiped, and everyone sang and danced and shared
the stories of our ancestors, while I delivered meals to
the sick patients in the hospital. It did not take me long
to discover that being a nurse was not the glamorous
job I had imagined. I would have given anything to
be with my people eating dry meat and muktuk—
delicious tiny cubes of whale blubber and skin.

If I could not go home, or even to the games, the least the nuns could do was continue to teach me. But of course, they did not.

While I was not the only child who did not go home that summer, I was lonely without Agnes. She was able to return home to her family, as they were now living in Tuktoyaktuk. But the nuns did their very best not to return any of us. Keeping us at the school was an easy way to ensure that we would return each fall, which was important to them. It wasn't just the chores—they were paid by the government per student, and plucking us from our homes and keeping us in their nests was a money-making business.

MY SUMMER SCHEDULE provided little time even for reading, and I was happy to have regular classes begin again in the fall. The Raven was nearly bearable in comparison with the long hours of chores and hospital work. But when the wind turned cold again in October, the whole of the North seemed to come down with a sickness called smallpox, and the hospital filled to capacity. Our classes were halted, once again, just weeks after they had resumed. Into November, as the hours of darkness lengthened day by day, we worked around the clock with the nuns and the men who were hired to do the chores that we children could not do. We were instructed to call these men Brothers, but they were far from being family. I was pretty sure that some did not even believe in God.

I was no stranger to hard work—life in the North required it—but I really disliked working in the hospital. The trappers were ill tempered and the sick women cried for their babies. Caring for them required so much of us that I longed for the return of the midnight sun to light the pages of my book, because I could only find a moment's peace to read very late in the evening. As it was, I held fairy tales and adventures to the window, desperate for escape, squinting in the darkness to catch the aquamarine glow of the northern lights.

See photo on page 97.

Many of my classmates fell ill eventually, tiny blistering sores rising on their skin and covering them

northern lights: curtains of light, often green or greenish-blue, seen near the magnetic North Pole, most visible at the equinoxes (March and September). Also known as aurora borealis.

with the same pox we had seen on the patients we attended. I no longer complained of the work. At least I did not have small-pox. As I watched several of the other children fall under the torment of the disease, I forgot both my exhaustion and my desire

to read, and worked hard to do what was necessary.

I had been emptying bedpans and basins of dirty cleaning water for many hours one day when my bladder started to hurt. I needed to hurry, but each time I made for the door, the Raven gave me another job to do. I pressed my bare knees together and shuffled from bed to bed, trying to ease the feverish patients. If only the pain would disappear, or the Raven would go away. My bladder grew heavier and heavier. I crossed my legs and tried not to think about it.

Just when I thought my whole tummy would burst, I noticed that the Raven was busy chastising Katherine.

I would have laughed out loud, if it had not meant I would pee myself. This was my chance, and I ran through the door. The hallway was like the tundra—it went on forever. No matter how far I traveled, I never seemed to get anywhere.

I was just one step from the doorway—when from out of nowhere appeared two hungry eyes, like those of an owl. They leveled themselves to the height of my nose. The mouth beneath them opened, baring fishy, yellow teeth, and instead of letting out an owly *whoooo*, the mouth growled. I felt something warm run down my legs, as the Brother ran off laughing.

See photo on page 98.

Before I could make it back to my room to clean myself up, the coarse voice of the Raven called after me. Her heels clicked and scraped against the floor, as she came closer. There was no escape.

"You are a filthy child," she said, when she saw what I had done.

I told her about the Brother, but she accused me of lying. To educate me, she left me shivering on the front lawn with a bucket of hot soapy water. I didn't

need to look up to know that the other girls would be looking through the window and laughing, while I washed out my canvas bloomers.

AS PEOPLE BECAME WELL again in late November, classes resumed. By then, I had read *Alice's Adventures in Wonderland* four times. Rosie had been telling the truth: Alice had not been hunting the rabbit at all. I would have brought its pelt back for my father.

One day, the Raven entered the classroom and told us that we would write letters home to our parents. I could hardly restrain myself in my seat. Not only did I long to make my father proud by telling him all that I had learned, and about all of the books I had read, but I wanted to ask him to come for me the next time the sun returned to melt the ice. We dipped our pens in our ink wells and wrote *Dear Mother and Father*, as instructed. For most of the students, the exercise was almost pointless. Many of their parents were unable to read English, just as my mother could not. Next we were told to write *I love it here at the school. The nuns have been very kind to us.*

Kind? That was a stretch. Instead, I wrote:

Dear Mother and Father,

I hate this school. You were right. The food is awful and the nuns are very mean. They won't even let me wear the stockings you bought for me. As you can see, I have already learned to read and write. Please, come to get me as soon as you can. I am ready to go home

Love,
Olemaun

I did not hear the rest of what the Raven dictated, but it didn't matter. I had written everything that I needed to say. I passed my letter to the front with the others.

Now, all I had to do was wait—or so I thought. Two days later, the Raven called me to her desk. "This is not what you were told to write," she said, tearing my letter in half and throwing it in the trash can. "Now, write it again, so it reads like this." She handed me a slip of paper to copy from.

The other children were dismissed to go and play in the recreation room, but I was held back to write my letter. I stared at the ceiling and imagined I was bundled in hides, safe in my father's dogsled, whizzing through a snowy valley of white. I counted the stars and watched the northern lights dance, frost clinging to my nostrils.

Sister MacQuillan glimpsed me through the door as she floated by. She stopped, stepped into the room, and looked over my shoulder.

"It's all right, Margaret," she said. "You may go to dinner now."

The Raven scowled at me when I handed in my letter. All I had written was, *Dear Mother and Father.* She would have held me there all night, had it not been for Sister MacQuillan, but it would not have mattered. Nothing could make me write that I loved the school.

I found a seat next to Agnes in the refectory. "What's wrong?" she asked.

"The Raven won't let me send a letter to my parents asking them to come and get me."

"Don't worry. I overheard two nuns talking today. Next week we are going over to CHAK to broadcast a message to our parents. You can tell them then."

CHAK was a new radio station that had been established in the North not long before I started school. My parents loved it. They would be listening.

The following week, we were marched over to the small wooden building in the middle of town and lined up outside in the dark. My knees nearly froze solid in the frigid winter air. Christmas was less than three weeks away. The nuns were crazy to make us children stand outside.

I had practiced and practiced what I intended to say, but when I stepped inside the warm building I was handed a piece of paper with writing on it. *Hello, Mom! Hello, Dad!* it read. *Merry Christmas! I miss you, but the nuns here treat us like family and school is very fun.*

See photo on page 98.

I did not know what the nuns thought they were going to accomplish with these messages home. The

63

false praise of the school would be lost on the many non-English-speaking parents.

"And if you do not say what you are told to, we will cut the transmission," the Raven informed me. "Is that clear?"

I should have known. Why would this message be any different?

I stood in front of the microphone. *Mother, Father, get me out of here, please. Take me home! I'm freezing and my teacher is wicked and mean*, I thought, but I said nothing. Not one word. I never stopped talking at home; my silence would surely tell them that something was wrong.

Chapter SIX

E VERY TIME A BLACKBOARD was to be cleaned or a floor mopped, the Raven was sure to put me to work doing it. I prayed that she would forget about me altogether, but her attentions only grew with the daylight hours. I returned to the dormitory one Saturday night in April, after an evening of the Raven's education. She was not pleased with my silence at the radio station and cleaning the nasty chicken coop was how she made me pay for it.

See photo
on page 99.

My raw fingers stung as I opened the door to an

explosion of excitement. Agnes was giddily twirling around her bed. She kicked up a leg to show me.

"New stockings," she chirped, as I pulled my own slouching pair back up over my knees. "Aren't they beautiful? I bet they belonged to a fancy Toronto lady. Everyone is getting new stockings!"

Maybe the outsiders had come to their senses: I might just survive another winter of the Raven's education if I could get my hands on some new stockings. I stripped off my old ones and threw them on the pile, praying for a nice black pair, like Agnes's. I closed my eyes and waited my turn.

The Raven swooped in. "I saved a special pair for you," she said.

I stared. I closed my eyes again and slowly opened them wider and wider. I looked to the other girls and examined their stockings, and then turned back to my own.

The Raven had played a heartless trick on me. Embarrassment and anger swelled in my heart. These stockings could never have belonged to a fancy lady from Toronto.

"They're… they're red!" I stammered.

The Raven cackled as I ran to my bed beneath the window. It was bad enough that I was much larger than the other girls, and that my calf muscles were far more pronounced than those of my skinny-legged classmates, but now I had to wear the only bright red stockings in the school. I pulled them on to see if they were really as bad as I thought. They were worse. The stockings made my legs look even bigger than they already were. I stared at my big fat red legs. I looked like a plump-legged circus clown.

The laughter of the other girls enveloped me. It wrapped a million fingers around me and would not let go. As soon as the Raven was gone, I pulled my favorite book from underneath my pillow and imagined the Raven in the role of the Queen of Hearts.

See photo on page 99.

THE NEXT MORNING, I crept into the refectory late, my calves on fire in those hideous stockings. A buzz filled the room and swarmed about the tables. I felt dizzy. Every eye was burning into my legs. I wanted to dissolve into my bowl of mush.

Katherine turned and pointed. "Fatty Legs," she laughed, bits of food spilling from her mouth.

"Fatty Face," I called back.

The Raven caught me by the ear. "If you cannot eat nicely with the other children, maybe you would be happier tending to the dirty laundry for the rest of the week," she said. "Now, get going. There's a fire waiting for you."

I could hardly will my feet to move under the weight of my big fat red legs, knowing that everyone was getting a good look at them as I sidled down the aisle and out the door of the dining hall.

My chest ached. As I stirred the dirty clothing, a tear escaped my eye. It fell from my chin onto the scalding cast iron vat.

Ptsch.

The tear bubbled and vanished with a poof of steam.

"Aha!" I whispered. In that moment, I knew how I would stop all of this Fatty Legs business.

I had only to await my chance.

FOR THE NEXT FEW DAYS, the other girls made sounds like the heavy beat of a drum when I walked by. *"Boom! Boom! Boom!"* they called.

They could go ahead and have their laugh at my expense. It would be short-lived. Although when they started calling Agnes "Skinny Legs," I felt like setting out across the ice and walking home, then and there. Katherine teased Agnes so mercilessly that one day, for the very first time, Agnes did not pick me first to be on her team at recreation time. My resolve hardened.

I could not lose my best friend.

The time had come to put my plan into action. Each morning as I pulled up my red stockings, my spirit rose. All I needed was opportunity.

On Sunday, my last day in the laundry room, it came. I looked around to make sure I was alone. The Raven usually went to her room after church to listen to the radio, and the Brother who helped to stoke the fire had gone out for a cigarette. I stripped off the stockings, and in one quick motion, shoved them into the blazing fire beneath the vat. The hideous things sizzled and crackled in the fire as they shrank before my eyes and vaporized into a thin wisp of smoke.

I smiled with satisfaction. I would not be bested. The Raven was about to find out what I was made of, and was she ever in for a shock.

She flailed like a fish on the ice when she noticed my bare legs, and threw her hands up in the air. "How dare you enter the refectory without your stockings? You will be dressed appropriately at all times. Now, go back and put them on this instant."

"I can't," I told her.

"And why not?"

"I just can't."

She could scream all she wanted. It wouldn't bring them back.

She rose from the table. "Margaret, you go back to your room and get those stockings, right now."

"They aren't there."

"Margaret Pokiak." Her beady black eyes bore holes into me. "I will find those stockings. Rest assured."

The hatchlings weren't giggling anymore. Everyone had to help in the search. We tore the crowded dorm room apart and scoured the whole school from top to bottom. We emptied our trunks and the nuns rummaged through our belongings. The Raven had each girl strip her bedding and flip her mattress.

"You had better tell her where those stockings are," Katherine said to me.

"Nope," I said. "No one's going to call me Fatty Legs, ever again."

"You think you're pretty brave, don't you?" She leaned forward and fixed her eyes on me, but I wasn't scared of her. I stood my ground.

"You *are* brave, Margaret," said Sister MacQuillan, stepping around the corner. Katherine moved away from me and rejoined the other Gwich'in girls. The Swan handed me a key. "Go and get your stockings from the storeroom."

Agnes met my eyes from where she stood over her upturned mattress and smiled.

It was time for lights out when I returned with the stockings. I would have to wait until the next morning to put them on.

When the morning came, I put on my beautiful thick pair of gray wool stockings. They were gorgeous. After our chores and prayers, I ran back up to the dormitory bursting with pride. I danced between the beds, whirling around for so long that I missed breakfast. I was eager to get to class on time, though. I sprang down the hallway stairs, like a gray-legged wolf.

The Raven choked on the claw she had been nibbling, as I strutted my sleek new legs past her desk.

Her face turned as red as seal's blood on snow. Sister MacQuillan stepped through the doorway and headed straight for the Raven. She whispered something in her ear, and the Raven blew up like a ptarmigan balloon. Her ears nearly popped off. Then Sister MacQuillan tilted her head gracefully in my direction. A faint smile crossed her lips. I knew the Raven would no longer be free to "educate" me as much as she had been.

The Raven thought she was there to teach me a few things, but in the end, I think it was she who learned a lesson: Be careful what birds you choose to pluck from their nests. A wren can be just as clever as a raven.

Chapter SEVEN

AT TIMES, I FELT as though my parents might forget me—forget that they had a daughter in a faraway school. And the dream returned often. The one in which I was trapped beneath the weight of the Raven's habit. I would never escape.

School ended, once again, and I soberly prepared for another summer of delivering meals to the sick and wishing I were back home. However, with the first boats came a new letter. It asked that I travel to Tuktoyaktuk on one of the school's boats. My family would meet me there. They wanted me to come home! The first time my father had written to me in English, it was to say he would not be coming for me. That letter had been painful to read. Now, at last, I could revel in each of the words he had penned on the page. I had not been forgotten. His letter proved it.

I couldn't wait to put the Raven at my back and some distance between us. The only outsider I would miss would be Sister MacQuillan. I could not leave without thanking her, so after I had packed my things, I went to her office.

"I am grateful for your kindness," I told her.

"You are a strong child. You will go far in life." She touched the top of my head and a tingle ran down to my toes. Then she pulled a book from her drawer and gave it to me. "I know how much you love this one."

It was my very own copy of *Alice's Adventures in Wonderland*. "Thank you," I said, taking the book and pressing it to my chest.

"You will be very missed, Margaret." She paused a

moment. Then she changed her words: "You will be very missed, Olemaun."

She had called me by my name—the name I had not heard in two years. Hearing it now brought tears to my eyes.

"Qugyuk," I said, pointing to her. It was the name I had always associated with her: Swan.

Sister MacQuillan elongated her neck and raised her arms like she would take flight. We both giggled.

I was sorry that I would not see the swan-like Sister again. I was sure that once I told my father about the Raven, he would never allow me to return to school.

See photo on page 100.

THE TRIP TO TUKTOYAKTUK aboard the Roman Catholic boat, the *Immaculata*, was crowded. We had no choice but to sit quietly as hour after hour drifted by and turned to day after day. The journey back to the ocean took much longer than the journey into the delta had because many children had to be dropped off on the way down the Peel and Mackenzie Rivers. Wherever the boat stopped, we children would scramble up the banks of the shore and run around wildly, stretching our legs and enjoying the space.

When we reached the mouth of the Mackenzie River, the saltwater smell of the bay unlocked distant memories and made me long for Banks Island. At that point, I was truly free of the outsiders' school. I had left it behind me, back past the tree line in a tangled cluster of waterways. After two long years, I was out on the open water, where I belonged. Each nightless day in that tiny boat had taken forever to pass. Now we were so close!

See photo on page 100.

We made our way across the bay to Tuktoyaktuk, and there was the *North Star,* anchored in the harbor. The moment was here at last. The *Immaculata* had only grazed the shore when I gave Agnes a quick hug and leaped from the boat. The Brothers couldn't stop me.

My father stood right there on the shore. He would have given them a what for if they had tried.

I was safe.

But my mother didn't know me.

"Not my girl," she told the Brothers. "Not *my* girl."

Those three words thudded between my ears, over and over, and I feared the Brothers would take me away with them again. I had not seen my mother in two years. She remembered a pale eight-year-old with pudgy cheeks. I was now tall, lean, very tanned, and ten years old.

My father knew me right away. He wrapped his arms around my body, and after a moment, so did my mother and siblings.

My mother had brought a small package of all of the things that I had liked to eat, assuming that I would be eager to try them once again. However, the food was strange and difficult to eat. It felt greasy and was salty, with a strong smell. I was not sure I would ever be able to eat it. My mother cried and said I was now an outsider. On the way to our camp, she asked my father to buy me some of their outsider-food from the Hudson's Bay store in Tuktoyaktuk. He laughed and told her that I was still Inuvialuit, and when I got hungry enough, I would eat. Eventually, I did.

See photo on page 101.

Before bed that first night, I read to my family from the book that Sister MacQuillan had given me. When I was done, I crawled under the warm hides, gazed at the glow of the embers from my father's pipe, and drifted off to sleep.

My curiosity had led me far away, and now here I was, after two years, satisfied that I now knew what happened to girls who went down rabbit holes.

After THE STORY

THE YEAR FOLLOWING MY return home was one of the happiest of my life. The excitement of hunting with my father, the pleasures of fishing with my mother, and the fun of seeking out goose eggs with my siblings all held new wonder for me. I was certain that I would not go back to the school in Aklavik for anything.

However, my three younger sisters grew curious. After they pestered my father non-stop, and the government made school attendance a condition for

See photo on page 101.

receiving child benefits, he gave in and agreed that they, too, could go and learn to read. I tried to warn them, just as Rosie had tried to warn me. Their hair would be cut, I told them. They would have to do many chores and kneel on their knees to ask for forgiveness. It was no use.

We Inuvialuit are headstrong. Thankfully, we are also resilient. So, reluctantly, I went with them—to make sure that they did not forget that wrens can be just as clever as ravens and owls.

The SCHOOLS

ABORIGINAL CHILDREN LIKE Margaret Pokiak learned many special skills that allowed them to cope with the natural environments they lived in. For example, by the time she was 10, Margaret could command her own dogsled team. As Europeans spread throughout North America, their quest to expand into new territories led them to seek ways to remove the people who already inhabited the land. One way of doing this was to send Aboriginal children to live at church-run schools where their traditional skills

See photo on page 102.

were replaced by those that would equip them to function in menial jobs. Though Margaret's parents knew better, some people believed that the schools would be good places to prepare their children for the rapidly changing world. Most children, however, were forcibly taken, some even kidnapped. The churches that ran the schools were paid a fee for each child attending, so they wanted to keep enrollment high. Just as Margaret had to work at the school in Aklavik, Aboriginal children throughout the North scrubbed floors, hauled water and firewood, made traps, worked traplines, or built furniture for sale. The schools were often overcrowded and dirty, and diseases such as tuberculosis were common. As well, the teachers were often unqualified to educate the children in their care.

See photo on page 102.

At the school in Aklavik, Margaret's clothing was taken away, her hair was cut, and she was not allowed to speak her language. The schools were meant to strip generation after generation of children of their culture and skills. In addition, children returning home were frequently considered outsiders. They could no longer speak their parents' languages, and they had lost their knowledge of the old ways. Furthermore, many children were abused at school, leaving wounds that could take generations to heal. They were then challenged to parent their own children, without having been parented themselves. In recent years, some residential school survivors have found the courage to speak out about what happened to them.

Today, the healing continues as many survivors, their children, and their children's children struggle to shed the shame of oppression and reclaim pride in their identities. Communities seek peace through healing circles, relearning their languages, participating in cultural celebrations such as traditional athletic games and powwows that showcase traditional dances, drumming, songs, and handicrafts, as well as through sharing their stories, philosophies, and inspirations in all forms of art and media—including books like this one.

Olemaun's SCRAPBOOK

Margaret and her family on the
five-day journey to Aklavik.
Margaret is second from the right.

*My older half-sister Ayouniq had
been plucked before I was born, but
we called her Rosie after her return.
In this photo, Rosie wears Inuvi-
aluit-style kamiks on her feet.*

Rosie turned, pulled apart the flaps of the tent door, and disappeared through the tunnel in the snow that formed the entrance to our home.

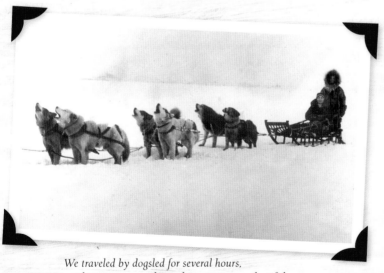

We traveled by dogsled for several hours, until we came to a place where game was plentiful.

Margaret and her
father sitting on top
of the schooner, the
North Star.

Margaret's mother

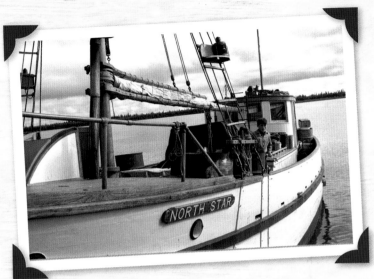

We traveled with six other schooners, each carrying as many as six or seven families. Our schooner was the North Star.

Beyond Tuktoyaktuk, the pingos rose out of the ocean like goose eggs with smashed-in tops. Pingos are formed when a large lump of ice pushes soil up to make a temporary mountain.

*We came to Reindeer Station, a settlement of herders,
and excitement consumed me.*

*We made our way down the plank and scrambled up the steep muddy slope to the
settlement our own great-grandfather, Old Man Pokiak, had founded as a trading
post. Margaret's great grandfather poses with his family in Aklavik, 1922. When
Margaret went to school, the houses in Aklavik were similar to this one.*

A tractor drives past the Hudson's
Bay Company store in Aklavik.

*Behind them stood two immense wooden buildings, so much larger than our schooner,
with rows and rows of windows. I had forgotten how big these buildings were.* This
photo, taken from the water, shows the school on the left and the hospital on the
right. In the school building, the boys' dormitory is on the left wing, while the
girls' dormitory is on the right. The classrooms are on the bottom floor.

An enormous photograph hung on one of the clean painted walls. In it, an outsider wore a fancy sash. Medallions like large coins hung from his chest—I would learn later that he was king of all of the outsiders. They told me he was also my king. This king is George VI, who ruled from 1936 to 1952.

Letters, like those from Rosie's books, decorated the walls of the classroom. I stared at them, trying to decipher what they might mean. This photo shows a classroom in the school that Margaret attended.

The nuns starched the peaks and the place where they shaved their heads underneath was sometimes visible.

An Anglican school room in Hay River, in the Northwest Territories, similar to the one Margaret sat in.

Even an outing like a trip to pick berries was tied to some sort of work. Because Margaret came from a treeless area, the berry bushes scared her.

Here, five of Margaret's sisters and her cousin play outside the hospital.

When the first boats began to appear, I could hardly believe the time had come. It would not be long before my parents arrived. In this photo, the community waits on the banks for the mail boats to arrive.

A nurse and patients in the Anglican hospital in Aklavik.
This hospital was similar to the one where Margaret worked.

The Brothers at Margaret's school dressed like the men in this photo.

A radio station similar to the one where Margaret refused to speak.

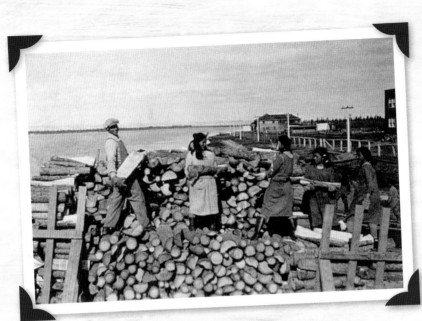

Margaret and other school kids hauling wood.

As soon as the Raven was gone, I pulled my favorite book from underneath my pillow and imagined the Raven in the role of the Queen of Hearts. Alice meets the Queen of Hearts.

The trip to Tuktoyaktuk aboard the Roman Catholic boat, the Immaculata, *was crowded.*

We made our way across the bay to Tuktoyaktuk, and there was the North Star, anchored in the harbor.

Margaret's brother Ernest, her father and mother,
with sisters Millie and Julia in front.

Here is a typical winter scene in Aklavik at the time
Margaret was a child.

Many Aboriginal children were sent to church-run schools. The girls in this picture boarded at an Aklavik school in the 1940s, the same time that Margaret went to school.

Margaret at 16, in an outfit she made herself.

Acknowledgments

THE AUTHOR WISHES TO thank everyone who helped to bring this story to print, including Robert N. Stephenson, Kate Messner, Judith Diehl, Stella Lisa Samuels, Maggie DeVries, Pam Robertson, and Laura Edlund. Thanks also to Annick Press.

Photo CREDITS

vi: (Olemaun and her sisters) courtesy of Margaret Pokiak-Fenton

2: basic map outlines by Map Resources. Additions by Lisa Hemingway.

88: (top, Pokiak family) Holman Photohist. and Oral History Research Cttee/NWT Archives/
N-1990-004: 0068; (bottom, Rose Pokiak) M. Meikle, Library and Archives Canada/PA-101772

89: (top, snow tent) R. Knights/NWT Archives/N-1993-002-0158; (bottom, dog sled) Frank and
Frances Carpenter collection, LC-USZ62-34903. Courtesy of Library of Congress Prints and
Photographs Division

90: (top and bottom, Margaret's father and mother) courtesy of Margaret Pokiak-Fenton

91: (top, *North Star* schooner) Wilkinson/NWT Archives/N-1979-051-1178; (bottom, pingo)
Hunt/NWT Archives/N-1979-062: 0008

92: (top, Reindeer Station) Canada. Affaires indiennes et du Nord/Library and Archives
Canada/PA-203204; (bottom, Old Man Pokiak) Jackson/NWT Archives/N-1979-004-0261

93: (top, Hudson's Bay store in Aklavik) K. Lang/NWT Archives/N-1979-007-0027; (bottom,
school and hospital) Fleming/NWT Archives/N-1979-050: 0042

94: (top, George VI) G. Eric and Edith Matson Photograph Collection, LC-DIG-matpc-14736.
Courtesy of Library of Congress Prints and Photographs Division; (bottom, classroom interior)
ECE/NWT Archives/G-1999-088:0142

95: (top, two nuns) Saich/NWT Archives/N-1990-003:0042; (bottom, school in Hay River)
YK Museum Soc./NWT Archives/N-1979-056-0057

96: (top, students on barge) Wilkinson/NWT Archives/N-1979-051-1191; (bottom, Margaret's
sisters and cousin) courtesy of Margaret Pokiak-Fenton

97: (top, waiting for the mail boat) J.L. Robinson/Library and Archives Canada/PA-102235;
(bottom, hospital) Fleming/NWT Archives/N-1979-050-0053

98: (top, brothers and boys) Sacred Heart Parish/NWT Archives/N-1992-255-0401; (bottom,
radio station) Wilkinson/NWT Archives/N-1979-051-0465S

99: (top, hauling firewood) courtesy of Margaret Pokiak-Fenton; (bottom, Alice and the
Queen of Hearts) illustration by Sir John Tenniel, scan © istockphoto.com/Darren Hendley

100: (top, the Immaculata) Library and Archives Canada/PA- 101292; (bottom, Tuktoyaktuk)
Dept. of the Interior/NWT Archives/G-1989-006:0082

101: (top, Margaret's parents, sisters, and brother) courtesy of Margaret Pokiak-Fenton;
(bottom, dog sled in Aklavik) Gar Lunney/National Film Board of Canada. Photothèque/
Library and Archives Canada/PA-163040

102: (top, school girls) Fleming/NWT Archives/N-1979-050-0954; (bottom, Margaret at 16)
courtesy of Margaret Pokiak-Fenton

105: (Christy Jordan-Fenton) courtesy of Allison Peck

Special thanks to the staff at NWT Archives, Library and Archives Canada, and the Brechin Group.

CHRISTY JORDAN-FENTON has been an infantry soldier, a pipeline laborer, a survival instructor, and a bareback bronco rider. Christy has also worked with street children. She was born just outside of Rimbey, Alberta, and has lived in Australia, South Africa, and the United States. Christy now lives on a farm near Fort St. John, British Columbia, where she and her husband are raising three small children, a few chickens, three dogs, a llama, two rabbits, and enough horses to outfit an entire town. Christy worked with her mother-in-law, Margaret Pokiak-Fenton, to write this story.

MARGARET POKIAK-FENTON was born on a tiny island far north of the Arctic Circle. She spent her early years on Banks Island; when she was eight years old she traveled to the mainland to attend the Catholic residential school in Aklavik, Northwest Territories. In her early twenties, while working for the Hudson's Bay Company in Tuktoyaktuk, she met her husband-to-be, Lyle, who was working on the DEW Line project. She followed him south to Fort St. John. Together they raised eight children. Margaret can be found most Saturdays at the local farmers' market, where she sells traditional Inuit crafts and the best bread and bannock in the North Peace.

LIZ AMINI-HOLMES spent her childhood daydreaming, drawing, reading, and writing in her family's backyard tree house. As an adult, she graduated from the Academy of Art College in San Francisco, California, with a BFA in Illustration. She now works as a freelance illustrator and her work has appeared in numerous publications, including children's books, and has been exhibited widely. She now lives in her own tree house in the San Francisco Bay Area with her husband, two children, and an ever-growing assortment of pets.